Father's Garden My Garden

Adapted from the teaching of

Ian Clayton

Printed in USA, UK and New Zealand
ISBN No. 978-1-911251-28-6

Acknowledgements

Son of Thunder Publications would like to thank Ian Clayton for his teaching and consultation in this book.
We would also like to thank Revelation Partners for the story and Patricia Ford for assistance.

Our special thanks goes to Anna Sophia for the paintings in this book.
annasophiasart.com

Alfred is alone. He is sad.

He does not want to play alone.

He throws a stick.

He kicks a rock.

There is a light.

He turns to look. There is a door.

He pushes and it swings open.

Alfred steps into the doorway

He sees grass and a garden.

It is warm and sunny.

There is a fatherly man. He sits on a bench.
The man smiles as Alfred walks up.

“Hello Alfred” says the man happily.

"Who are you?" Asks Alfred.

"I am the Father of this garden in Heaven" says the man.

Alfred felt happy to be there.

“No one likes me” says Alfred.

“I like you Alfred” says the Father.

“I made this garden, and you are always welcome” says the Father.

“Can I look around?” Asks Alfred

“Your angel friends are waiting for you” says the Father.

Alfred plays with them all day.
He feels very happy!

"Can I come here again?" asks Alfred.

"Yes you can - we are here every day
with the Father"
the angels say.

“I had a really good time!” Says Alfred. He gives the Father a hug.

“I do not want to go” He says sadly.

“This is your garden Alfred.
You can come back when you want”

Says the Father.
“That is great!” Says Alfred.
“Can I bring my friends?”
“Yes you can.” Says the Father.

“I will come back soon. I like being with you!”

Alfred waves to the Father.

Father's Garden My Garden

Coloring Book

Being Alone

Being Bored

Stepping In

Meeting Father

Talking to Father

Fun with Father

Angels

Father's Garden - My Garden

Eden

Waving Goodbye

Draw your own angels

Draw your own garden